Milly the Meerkat

Written by Oakley Graham

Licensed exclusively to Top That Publishing Ltd
Tide Mill Way, Woodbridge, Suffolk, IP12 1AP, UK
www.topthatpublishing.com
Copyright © 2014 Tide Mill Media
All rights reserved
0 2 4 6 8 9 7 5 3 1
Manufactured in China

Written by Oakley Graham
Illustrated by Alexia Orkrania

All rights reserved. No part of this publication may be reproduced, stored in
a retrieval system, or transmitted in any form or by any means, electronic,
mechanical, photocopying, recording or otherwise, without the prior written
permission of the publisher. Neither this book nor any part or any of the
illustrations, photographs or reproductions contained in it shall be sold or disposed
of otherwise than as a complete book, and any unauthorised sale of such part
illustration, photograph or reproduction shall be deemed to be a breach of the
publisher's copyright.

ISBN 978-1-84956-304-8

A catalogue record for this book is available from the British Library

For Noah

Milly the Meerkat

Written by Oakley Graham

For Noah

There once was a young meerkat called Milly, who was bored as she sat on an earth mound taking her turn as lookout.

To amuse herself, Milly took a great, big breath and barked out, 'Snake! Snake! A snake is approaching the baby meerkats' burrow!'

All the other meerkats came running out of their own burrows to help Milly drive the snake away.

But when they arrived at the top of the mound, they found no snake. Milly laughed at the sight of their angry faces.

'Don't bark "snake", Milly,'
said the other meerkats,
'if there's no snake!'

Later that day, Milly was feeling even more bored and barked out again, 'Snake! Snake! A snake is approaching the baby meerkats' burrow!'

To her mischievous delight, Milly watched as the other meerkats rushed to the mound to help her drive the snake away.

But when the other meerkats arrived at the top of the mound, they found no snake. Again, Milly laughed at the sight of their angry faces. 'Don't bark "snake", Milly,' repeated the other meerkats, 'if there's no snake!'

Late in the afternoon,
Milly saw a REAL
snake slithering
close to the baby
meerkats' burrow.

Alarmed, Milly leapt to her feet and barked out as loudly as she could, 'Snake! Snake! A snake is approaching the baby meerkats' burrow!'

But the other meerkats just thought that Milly was trying to fool them again, so they didn't come out to help her.

Outside, as day turned to night, everyone wondered why Milly hadn't returned for supper. They went to look for Milly and found her crying on top of the lookout mound.

'There really was a snake here! The meerkat babies have scattered! I barked out, "snake" as loudly as I could,' sobbed Milly. 'Why didn't you come to help me?'

A wise, old meerkat tried to comfort Milly
as they walked back to the village.
'We'll help you look for the lost meerkat babies,'
he said, putting his arm around Milly.

'You have learnt an important lesson today, Milly.
Nobody believes a liar ... even when they are
telling the truth!'

The entire meerkat colony helped Milly look for the lost babies and once they were all found, they tucked them up safely in their burrows.

Milly was very sorry for what she had done and promised that she would never lie to her family and friends again.

More great picture books from Top That Publishing

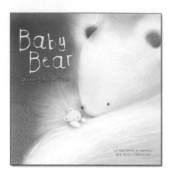

ISBN 978-1-84956-120-4

Baby Bear tentatively explores the wonders of the outside world.

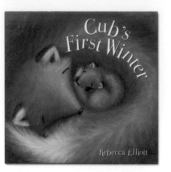

ISBN 978-1-84956-099-3

An inquisitive fox cub experiences the onset of his first winter.

ISBN 978-1-84956-303-1

Snuffletrump the piglet will try anything to get rid of his hiccups!

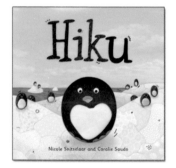

ISBN 978-1-84956-073-3

Can you find Hiku as he sneaks away from an important family visit?

ISBN 978-1-84956-305-5

The animals are making a hullabaloo in this humorous picture storybook!

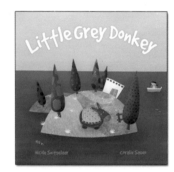

ISBN 978-1-84956-245-4

Unique illustrations capture the loving bond between two best friends!

ISBN 978-1-84956-304-8

Milly the meerkat learns a very important lesson in this classic tale.

ISBN 978-1-84956-302-4

Follow the antics of the escaped zoo animals as they cause pandamonium!

ISBN 978-1-84956-101-3

Enjoy the beautiful moments between a mother cat and her kitten.

ISBN 978-1-84956-100-6

Comic wordplay explores what a toucan or toucan't do.

Available from all good bookstores or visit www.topthatpublishing.com
Look for Top That Apps on the Apple iTunes Store